Buggerall

Jon Tregenna

Tregni Books

Tregni

First published in the UK in 2010 by Tregni Books
23 Coleshill Terrace, Llanelli, SA15 3BT

info@tregni.co.uk

Copyright 2010 Jon Tregenna

Second edition 26.05.10

ISBN: 978-1-4452-8171-1

Jon Tregenna has asserted his right under the Copyright, designs and Patents Act. 1988 to be identified
as the author of this work.

Tregni Limited Reg No. 5627013

~~~~

Buggerall

Buggerall is a modern take on Dylan Thomas' *Under Milk Wood* and, like the original, can be performed as a 'play for voices' with a cast of five, or as a full-scale stage production.

The author would like note his appreciation for Peter Thabit Jones, Carmarthenshire Council, Christopher J. Rees, Jill Stevens and Llanelli Youth Theatre for their help in bringing this play to life.

Jon Tregenna

Jon was educated at Llanelli Boys Grammar School. He spent the 80s in Cardiff working as an actor and the 90s in bands in London. Since moving back home to Wales Jon has written episodes of *The Bench* and *Belonging* for the BBC and created and co-wrote the award winning S4C comedy drama series *Cowbois Ac Injans* with his sister, Catherine Tregenna. Jon has written two stage plays, *Buggerall*, and *The Prince Of Wales*, and produces the online comedy drama *David Garland Jones*. He was the singer/songwriter for Welsh pop group *The Mams* and has had his poetry published in *The Seventh Quarry*.

At the time of publication Jon worked as an attendant at the Dylan Thomas Boathouse in Laugharne.

Buggerall

ACT ONE

[Darkness. Light up on TYPO, sitting staring at a laptop. A copy of Under Milk Wood visible. Some rubbish strewn around – evidence of work avoidance – food wrappers, cans etc.]

TYPO: 'Seaside town life in South Wales has changed greatly since the middle of the last century. Gone are many of the small businesses the great poet celebrated. Gone perhaps is that unchanging way of life passed down from generation to generation. A question is now posed – what if the poet was alive and well and writing about life in a West Wales seaside town today? What would he make of amusement parks and hen nights, traffic wardens and satellite TV, UPVC and lottery, plastic milk bottles, windsurfers, ipods, jet-skis and mobile phones: a world where a Blackberry… is no longer a fruit.

The butchers, the bakers, the walking stick makers; high class drapers and watch repairers; men selling fish out of wheelbarrows around pubs with snugs, and tapping barrels for free beer and grinning, and quarrymen quarrelling, and old sea dogs with salty stories and sweet tobacco in all their pipes: all gone. The clockmakers is now a gift shop. The chapel: a private house. The cobblers: a surf shop. The dairy: a car park.'

Pretty good.

'And yet… the landscape and location dictate a sense of timelessness. Narrow your eyes and sense the town's histories, secrets and intrigues. Hear old fashioned sounds in the warm late summer air as snip-snip goes the silver scissors at Scissor Sisters hair salon, formerly the drapers. The proprietor? Eve Edwards.'

EVE: This woman who came in this morning - 23 hairs on her head. I counted them: 23. She asked for a shampoo and set. I said – 'What's the name above the door say, love? Paul Daniels?*'   [*US version – 'David Blaine']

TYPO: 'Hear the curlew cry, kitten creak and siren shriek – not the cockle factory hooter of old, but a skittish car alarm. And now a rusty squeak as an aged tartan shopping trolley trundles into the square - this one not loaded with broad beans and tinned tongue, but with flyers for a new supermarket - 12 miles away and a free bus on Fridays'

LAZY LOTTIE: One more street then I'll dump them. In the recycling bin, mind…
I'm environ-mental.

TYPO: 'And hear the door-to-door salesman's footstep on cobblestone and the rat-a-tat of signet ring on door frame.'

SALESMAN: Are you aware that Gaslec Direct can save you 23% on your bill? Let me show you an independent survey, Mrs… er…

JILL JOG: Sod off, will you?

LAZY LOTTIE: Excuse me. Are you going to every house in the village…?

SALESMAN: Yes. Why?

LAZY LOTTIE: Take these flyers round for me? Go on, save my feet.

TYPO: 'And hear the ancient cry of the all-seeing bin-scavenging gulls and the old bronze bell sending children cheering victoriously out of temporary classrooms into the school yard, in a uniformed haywire tumble.'

SCHOOL GIRLS [sing]: *Who wants a boyfriend?*
No not me
Coz they always smell of pee
They murdered my hamster
And they broke my CD player
And they steal all our Barbies
To play Buffy Vampire Slayer

TYPO: 'The damp maligned boys play a game of their own invention. A game called Harry Potter and the Half-Blood Prince.'

BOYS: Whey!

TYPO: 'Or Pirates Of The Caribbean: At Worlds End.'

BOYS: Whey!

TYPO: 'Or X-Men Origins - Wolverine.'

BOYS: Whey!

TYPO: 'The subtle variations not immediately apparent to the untrained eye.'
            [beat] The films are pretty similar too…

SCHOOL GIRLS *[sing]*:   *Who wants a boyfriend?*
                             No not me
                             Coz they're stupid as can be

TYPO :   'And hear the optimistic clip-clop tip-tap tat of cheap high heels strutting
            out, and the traditional melancholy chime of the MOT-free ice cream
            van. Hear the sonic jet-ski roar; the chirruping mobile phone evensong;
            bingo-call, crow cry and karaoke. Somewhere tonight somebody will
            murder Frank Sinatra to polite applause.'

DRUNKEN DUNCAN: *'Start spreading the news…'*

TYPO: 'However, evidence still remains of an age now gone. See the cast iron
            boot scraper, war memorial, Celtic cross, milk churn stand and decaying
            fishing boat marooned forever on the silted channel. See the last few
            original sash windows holding out against the cruel chill sea wind, the
            pared down petrol pump and the local place-names with origins long
            forgotten… See the travelling fair that diesels and cranks into the village
            every year, with its crippled Crooked House, emaciated goldfish and
            blunt darts. And Lover's Lane, forever Lover's Lane.'

ROSE: I could get pregnant.

BOYO: You can't. Not the first time.

TYPO: 'And here in this echo of another time town, front steps are still scrubbed
            by god-fearing ladies in pinafore and hair-net.'

DOOLALLY SAL: Bless this godless town oh Lord, and keep the boys with
                    their trousers too big for them and the knicker-showing girls
                    from stealing my wheelie-bin. Amen.

TYPO: When's the deadline…? Three days time. Ok. Focus… Can't
                    sit here doing buggerall. Friends mock - they say I've been
                    doing buggerall for years… But my mind is mulling,
                    waiting… open to imagination, open to distraction too, yet
                    always striving for one luminous strand. But buggerall
                    comes.

TYPO:	Here on an afternoon in an ordinary town by the extraordinary sea, the night before the annual Boat Club Fun Day…
RUGBY LADS:	Whey!
TYPO:	And nothing comes. Listening to the lads setting off for the rugby club to line their stomachs in preparation for tomorrow's drinking.
RUGBY LADS:	Whey!
TYPO:	And nothing comes. To begin…? Make a coffee…? It could be a long night... No. Start first.
	'To begin… To begin at the…'
	I can hardly begin at the beginning can I? To begin at the... End? Ha! *(thinks)* Then again…
	'In a dimly lit bar of a pub not yet open for evening trade, two young men sit at a table, waiting. There is a third chair, empty. One man, Simon: lost in thought. Another, Grom: bored, restless, has an idea. He mimes throwing a matchbox over a pint glass – although he has neither.'
GROM:	Yes. Four fingers… You. Four fingers. The matchbox has landed on its end, which equals, 'You drink four fingers of your pint.'
SIMON:	I'm aware of the rules of the Matchbox Game.
GROM:	Good. Four fingers. Go on.
SIMON:	However, we haven't actually got any drinks. Surely a pre-requisite for any successful 'drinking' game.
GROM:	So? Haven't got a matchbox either. Your turn. Pretend! Something to do. Whilst we… wait.
TYPO:	Again Grom tosses the imaginary matchbox into the air.

GROM: Two fingers… Me. I drink two fingers of beer.

SIMON: You're going to play it on your own?

GROM: Won't be the first time.

SIMON: With no drink or matchbox?

TYPO: The futility of his actions recognised, Grom's attention starts to wander. He senses they are not alone…

GROM: Weird, mun… Sort of staring. Do they know why we're here? Do they know why they're here? *[beat]* That one… looks a bit… simple.

SIMON: You're in no position to judge…

GROM: Thank you very much.

TYPO: The already dim light flickers.

GROM: I don't want to go.

TYPO: Grom passes Simon the imaginary matchbox, but it is ignored. He is insistent and so the invisible item is reluctantly taken. Grom gestures - play the game! Play the bloody game! Simon humours him, and Grom watches expectantly for the outcome.

SIMON: It landed in my pint.

GROM: Yes! Down in one!

TYPO: But let's not get ahead of ourselves… Let's go back a short while. The same pub. One day earlier. It is Simon Saddlers's stag night and three men play the matchbox game as it was intended to be played: with real beer and a real matchbox. Said matchbox floats in Simon's pint.

CARL: Yes!

GROM: The rules state, sir, that you have to drink that pint down in one.

CARL: Rules are rules.

GROM: C'mon, have a laugh, innit? Enjoy!

SIMON: Shh. I just want a quiet night, ok? I promised Belle.

CARL: It's tradition. Last night of freedom. Do something disgraceful and humiliating that'll haunt you forever.

SIMON: No. I'm not licking cream from a strippogram's navel, or being tied to the lifeboat memorial. No silly top shelf cocktails, no yards of ale, and definitely no wrestling.

GROM: What we gonna do then? That's everything!

BELLE: It's your stag night. Enjoy. I intend to have a damn good hen night. Don't look so worried. I love you.

SIMON: *[to BELLE]* Ditto. I mean… Me too. *[to CARL and GROM]* I want no mucking about. It's important… end of an era and all that. Time to be responsible.

CARL: Yeah, right. You'll never change.

GROM: When's the stripper coming?

SIMON: You haven't? I told you. I'll have none of it. I'll leave.

CARL: I didn't book one.

GROM: Aw.

CARL: Well, well… Simon Saddler, retired playboy.

SIMON: Where you going?

CARL: Need some fresh air.

TYPO: Outside the pub Carl, thwarted, approaches a police woman, fake.

CARL: Sorry love, you're not needed.

STRIPPOGRAM: I want paying, mind. I can't be being messed around.

CARL: *[to audience]*   She'd have stripped. Simon would have performed. Like he does. Click. Click. Hey Belle, this is a photo of the man you're marrying… didn't know whether to tell you or not. *[beat]* Here's twenty quid for your trouble.

STRIPPOGRAM: I don't mind if it's out here. I'll keep my bra on if he's shy.

CARL: It's ok. G'night 'officer'. *[to audience.]* I wouldn't really have done that...

STRIPPGRAM: The cabbies look at me in their mirrors wondering where they've seen me before. It's worst of all when a distant relative or school friend wonders where they know this half-dressed, half-alive, half dead lipstick face from. I make £50 a call out with a discount for pensioners.

TYPO: The landlords don't mind, so long as the lads drink and she doesn't get foam on the furniture.

STRIPPOGRAM: Evening lads.

RUGBY LADS: Whey-hey! Get 'em off!

STRIPPOGRAM: In my own time.

TYPO: In a museum-piece Formica kitchen clasping a bible she hasn't read for years, Doolally Sal says a prayer.

DOOLALLY SAL: Save me from the buggers and the muggers and the young fraudsters with fake plastic identity cards. I'm protected by God, and the crows up my chimney-breast nesting watch over me. Save me from being knocked down at dawn by tattooed cold cockle-men in Landrovers; the rocket booming noise from the cars of boys in caps; the crying babies of underage mums, and loud drinking men cussing in the early evening summer sun.

DRUNKEN DUNCAN: Damn you sun. You're making me thirsty.

TYPO:	At home, Drunken Duncan's wife, Jill Jog, gets ready for her evening exercise with her two jovial jogging companions. They sit in the kitchen like three king-sized Pot Noodles.
JILL JOG:	We'll go up the hill towards the chapel.
LAZY LOTTIE:	Hill? Noo! My calves are aching from last time. Let's go on the flat. And then back. Not too far. Then fish and chips. With mayonnaise.
CAROL COMMODE:	We had a to-do at the old people's home today. This woman had a knife.
LAZY LOTTIE:	What kind of knife? Carving knife?
JILL JOG:	Machete?
CAROL COMMODE:	86 she is, right. And she was going to kill this 85 year old man. Stab him. She said he wanted to write her a poem or something daft. Anyway, she's brandishing this… well, butter knife it was, but sharp enough… above her head, like this… Staff were running, panicking, getting towels and sedative. I saw all this, and I walked up to her and I put a fork in her other hand. And she sat straight down and asked, 'What's for tea?' She did!
JILL JOG:	I could do with some tea. And a sausage roll. After the jog…
TYPO:	The trail of ale begins in the smoke-free body odour air of the Old Red Lion, the town's last remaining pub of any character where beer is still served in large jugs straight from the barrel. The three young men follow the well-worn flag-stoned tracks to the old mahogany bar where ranks of workers and farmers and fishermen plotted and drank for a century or more… And in more recent times, women, liberated by factory work and magazines, smoked and danced with abandon as the church organist pulled his cap down to his eyes to disguise himself, and rattled out the devil's own jazz on the pub piano…

TYPO:	And in a black frame by the ticking mantle clock, two handsome flat capped black and white dead drunks frown down - their likeness captured a hundred years back by a travelling hack; just two of many thousands of departed drinkers, immortalised and nameless forever.
CARL:	Hey boys, let me take a photo of you two. Say… 'big jugs'!
GROM/SIMON:	Big Jugs!
GROM:	*[to audience member]* Big jugs, the ones they serve beer in… Not… I know what you were thinking! Ach y fi!
CARL:	I'll put the photo on facebook when I get home...
TYPO:	Says Captain Carl, celebrated captain of the local pool team. Eight ball genius/
SIMON/GROM:	/One and the same!
TYPO:	But a loser in love…
SIMON/GROM:	One and the same!
TYPO:	Plays an elaborate trick shot and wins the game.
GROM:	Contribution for Simon's stag night tab. It's not for me. Keep it quiet tho'. Yeah? Any shrapnel in your purse? Thanks very much.
SIMON:	I'm a complicated man. I look at simple things, and before my eyes they tangle in a whirl of knots.
CARL:	I'm a simple man. I do exactly what it says on the tin.
GROM:	I don't go for that self analysis crap. I've thought about it, and how I think about myself… and it's not for me. I don't think so anyway.
SIMON:	Things that are good for me, I let them wither away. I find myself unable to care… in here. I want to care about me, my future, my girl… I want to cling to her and be happy.

TYPO:	Belle and Eve cluck and preen and prepare for the hen night. Belle wears a veil, some 'L' plates and has ribbons in her hair.
EVE:	Want a ciggie?
BELLE:	No. Not good for the baby.
EVE:	I know that... Sorry. Am I bad?
SIMON:	I want Belle to look at me and feel proud, and want me to kiss her and not want to kiss anyone else. I want a better job so I can earn more money and maybe move away from this safe little world of mine. I'm getting married next week. I need it. I really think I need it. I'm sure I really think I need it...
BELLE:	I can't wait to get married. It's what people like me and people like him do, innit? We come from tidy homes. Clean and tidy. And I'm 22 and he's 26, so we're not kids anymore. And it's not like this town would hold the most successful Brad Pitt look-a-like competition, coz, well... no-one round here looks like him. And as for brains...well... but Simon's a bit different... Not that different, but different enough. He knows how to hold a girl/
SIMON:	/I'm at that stage of life where I need responsibility.
BELLE:	He always talks over me/
SIMON:	/Shot, Grom!
BELLE:	And I tell him to listen and he does this concentrating face, like he's building a house of cards; like if he doesn't focus, it'll collapse. He tries to look calm but his feet keep tapping under the table. Feet ready to run/
SIMON:	/Life is spinning by, and I'm acting like a fifteen year old, happy with a can of Diamond White, sneaking kisses and owning nothing except my massive TV, and I watch too much of it in our one and a half bed mid-link plywood creaking house. And I see the cracks where the wall meets the ceiling, and the litter blows into my garden, only my garden, nobody else's, just mine... Why is that? And I could repair the cracks. I could. I'd borrow the tools. I have the skills. I was bred with the skills.

SIMON: Genetically I have the skills for minor household tasks. Because in my genes I have the means to build boats and bridges and plough fields and scrape coal from the wet dark and fashion a fine leather saddle... and discover continents. It's in my bones – and these hands whose shape I share with dead craftsmen - hands that carved bardic chairs and wrote eisteddfod-winning poetry and yet my job is so 'now' and so... useless... and so parasitic...

You ever had an accident sir?... Madam?... You sir... any accidents at work...? No win no fee... Any of your family or friends...? You sir, slipped on any wet leaves? Tripped on a loose paving stone? Fallen down a manhole, sir? Eaten by lions, madam? *[beat]* I see our local postman. He catches my eye - dog-bites, falling slates, wet leaves, booby trap letter-bombs: a good prospect! Sir, I work for an accident claims company – No Win No Fee...

STANLEY POSTMAN: I did slip on a grape once, in Tescos, Carmarthen...

CAROL COMMODE: What's this? You haven't signed anything?

STANLEY POSTMAN: I haven't! I didn't! I mustn't!

CAROL COMMODE: Get lost, yeah? Changing from gas to 'lectric, and telephones from the bloody gas board. I'm sick of it. Up to here.

SIMON: No, no... this is Accident Claims.

CAROL COMMODE: Same difference... harassing people. It's all a con.

SIMON: Yeah. Yeah. So I was here just doing a job, trying to earn a few quid... being pleasant I thought... But no... I'm conning people! Right! Fine. OK! ANYONE WANT TO BE CONNED? STEP RIGHT UP! RIGHT THIS WAY!!

GROM: I fund my dope habit with shop-lifting. Sometimes I fund it through dealing. Posh kids down here in the summer in their camper vans with money to burn.

SURFER: I am a surfer, mad with drugs.

GROM: When I was a kid I used to love the sea. My dad and I went out in the bay once in his old wooden boat with a little cabin where we drank tea from a plastic flask and ate cream crackers. Nothing else mattered. He left when I was seven. I knew good from no good; right from wrong. I chose no good. I chose wrong. I always had something to blame.

CARL: I got seven GCSE's. Only I had passed any. I felt like I'd failed my friends.

GROM: I've just nicked three baby's romper suits. Easy to sell. So I can buy my rounds. Got to pay my way… Ah… Must dash.

SECURITY GUARD: Stop thief!

TYPO: Shouts the pursuing security guard, but as the thief makes his getaway Simon dabs out the toe of his big black boot and the security guard slides along the polished tiled floor of the shopping centre, like a bison on ice.

SIMON: Sorry, mate. You ok?

CAROL COMMODE: Maybe he wants to make a claim.

SIMON: The manholes are sealed. The pavements are flat. The lions are tame. I feel my brain crying and I can't move…

EVE: This girl came into the Salon. Right vain thing, she is. She told me she was thinking of having a mole removed. I told her… 'They're a swine. They make holes all over your garden.' And I had that Mrs Jones Little Bit in again today for a haircut.

BELLE: What did she have done?

EVE: The sides. Last week it was the fringe, just a...

MRS JONES LITTLE BIT: Little bit off the front.

EVE: I can't charge for that. It's only a minute it takes. But today it's…

MRS JONES LITTLE BIT: A little bit off the sides, just a little bit.

EVE: Two weeks ago it was a little bit off the back. Nowhere else, just the back. I can't charge for that, can I? Then, next week it'll be…

MRS JONES LITTLE BIT: Little bit off the top. Tiny little bit.

EVE: I realised now - every four weeks she gets a free haircut.

GROM: £10 for the three… I nicked them especially for you. They'd cost you £20 in the shops!

SIMON: /I don't want my baby in stolen clothes, ok?

GROM: The baby won't know!

SIMON: No. I want to give a good example.

CARL: You?!

SIMON: I'm looking forward to bonding with my boy. I'm good with kids. My eight year old nephew thinks I'm great. He asked me to his birthday party last week. I didn't make it.

CARL: Course.

SIMON: I was really tempted though – chocolate factory, McDonalds and a sleepover. But I think he's got nits.

GROM: Do you know what I hate. When people use capital letters to text you. I mean it's like they're shouting innit? 'C U THERE. WHAT TIME?' Use little letters innit? More calming.

[SIMON's mobile phone rings]

GROM: 'Hello? This is Simon Saddler' phone, he's not here at the moment, can I take a message?

SIMON: Fool! Give me my phone!

GROM: Uh-huh… No worries… *[The call ends]* What's the best pint you ever had? Carl? Best pint?

CARL: White Horse, Greenwich Village, New York.

GROM: Yeah, yeah, posh git. I've only been across the Loughor Bridge three times. And one of those was by accident. Wrong bus. Drunk.

GROM: Lost my anorak. And a shoe… Broke a rib. Fell in a river… Got bitten by an eel. *[beat]* At least, I think it was an eel.

SIMON: What did they say?

GROM: My best pint is this one, right here, right now. With my best mates.

SIMON: Who was on the phone, mun?!

GROM: Your boss. You've been sacked. Shouting at people. Like a mad thing apparently.

CARL: Unemployed, skint and about to be a dad!

GROM: The Welsh way!

SIMON: Not funny.

GROM: Sorry. These baby clothes… have them for nothing.

SIMON: Cheers mate.

TYPO: Outside on Quay Street on my way to the store for some inspiration and a packet of crisps I see the sad scuffed shapeless shape of Drunken Duncan, the window un-cleaner limping up his heavy wooden ladder smelling of last night's Guinness, and putting more dirt on the window than he takes off.

DRUNKEN DUNCAN: I love beer, me. But I'm never drunk tho'.

JILL JOG: Last night you came in, you swore at the kids, ate four Findus Crispy Pancakes and fell asleep in front of the shopping channel. QVC I think it was. Review of the day.

DRUNKEN DUNCAN: Did I? And what did I do then?

JILL JOG: You woke up and bought me a Lapus Lazuli ring for £25.64 plus postage.

DRUNKEN DUNCAN: Not on my Visa card? It's full to the brim.

JILL JOG: No, love. On mine. You old sod you!

GROM:	Starving, me. Got a scotch egg from my mum's shop. Two days out of date.
TYPO:	He peels off the meat which he places in an empty glass.
SIMON:	What are you doing?
GROM:	I don't like the meat bit.
CARL:	Why don't you just boil an egg? Or eat a pickled one?
GROM:	No, no. I like the scotch ones.
SIMON:	Let's go for a walk…
GROM:	Walk?
SIMON:	Come on, it's a beautiful night and it's my do.
GROM:	'Walk' though?

[beat – SIMON indicates smoking a spliff.]

GROM:	Ah! A 'walk' walk!
CARL:	I'll buy some cans.
TYPO:	Alright lads?
GROM:	We're going for a 'walk'.
TYPO:	A walk?
GROM:	A 'walk' walk!
TYPO:	Ah!
GROM:	Coming with us?
TYPO:	Nah.
SIMON:	Why not? You got buggerall to do.

TYPO:	Exactly. I've only popped out to get supplies in. Take care lads.
SIMON:	Nos da.
TYPO:	And the boyos head down to the graveyard to get stoned off their heads by the headstones of the dead.
BELLE:	Do I have to have the condoms on? Looks a bit common.
EVE:	Its tradition, gal! Got some plans for you. You've got to sell a one month old Evening Post. Got to snog a ginger man. Got to put a pair of y-fronts on over your tights, and you got to find a man with shell-suit trousers by the bar and when he picks up his pint you got to pull his trousers down. And hope he's got pants on.
BELLE:	God help me. A ginger man?
TYPO:	Our likely lads head across town towards the old chapel, now home to a family from London who love the area so much they visit at least twice a year.
VIOLA:	I have a passion for painting, and an even bigger passion for my painting tutor. I learnt some Welsh so I could fit in at the local shop on our visits. Nice to fit in. But no bugger speaks it there. My husband is local. His name is Geraint. My parents could never pronounce it - 'Gay-rye-ant.'
GERAINT:	My family were originally from the area. I was born here, but it was different then. Less Nike and Pepsi and somehow more bohemian and more intelligent. Less 'logo' and more 'boho' if you like! *[expecting a laugh]* Oh… that always gets a laugh in Richmond. Viola and I came down for my 50th and saw that the chapel was for sale, and we were really lucky to get it. Fortunately I had a 'word' with the estate agent.
VIOLA:	A £500 word, but it was worth every penny.
GERAINT:	Apparently local people were hoping to turn it into a community facility: meeting place, table tennis, rehearsal rooms, that kind of thing… but I got the nod from the planning department/

VIOLA: /For a small fee/

GERAINT: /That drug users were to come here for advice and treatment?! It's
                far too beautiful for that.

VIOLA: And our children love it here. It's so peaceful for us when
                they're down by the bay, far away.

[SOUND – jet-skis blasting past]

TOWNSFOLK: SHUT-UP!!

GERAINT: You see, before we bought the place we sent the kids out on the
                jet-skis, and do you know what? You can't actually hear them
                from the chapel.

SIMON: It's a beautiful night. Look at the stars. There's The Plough.

GROM: Will your dad give us free chips?

SIMON: No. And stop asking him.

GROM: He's got a shop-full, mun.

CARL: Orion's Belt.

SIMON: They're the only two anyone ever knows. One day I'm going to
                learn them all.

GROM: Isn't that the reverend?

[SIMON and CARL stare at the sky.]

SIMON: Which one is that?

GROM: The old man by the gates.

CARL: What gates? Can you see gates?

SIMON: What gates?

GROM: The church gates.

CARL: Ah! That's Reverend Peacock. 91 years old, skin as thin as a
                   communion wafer. He christened me. He seemed ancient then.

GROM: I stopped going to church when I was 6 – 'Jesus wants me for a
                   sunbeam'. Not me he doesn't...

VIOLA: Who's that funny old man by the gate?

GERAINT: I'll tell him to go away. Excuse me!

CARL: Rev! They closed the chapel down mate! It's an 'ouse now!

REVEREND: This place was full when I was young
                               When my faith had just begun
                               But at this old age I wonder why
                               My faith has failed to satisfy

                               My congregation dead and gone
                               My chapel closed to prayer and song
                               My sermons Lord, were far too long
                               And my faith has failed to soldier on...
                               Yet I pray that I'll be proven wrong

DOOLALLY SAL: He took me on a date once, the young reverend. I was 14.
                               We had bicycles. I was so excited! It was the best day of my
                               life. Then he married someone else. I never knew what I did
                               wrong. Something, I suppose. Maybe he preferred her face
                               to mine. Skin like an old boiled hen. Eyes with no colour.
                               No lips left for lipstick. They were full and warm once. I
                               wonder what kissing is like?

EVE: She comes in my salon. Dresses like 1970's curtains. She has funny
                   turns. One time she keeled over. We called the paramedics, they put this
                   oxygen mask on her. She lifted it up to put her scarlet lipstick on/

DOOLALLY SAL: /Just in case...

SIMON: Think of all the people that have been married, or christened, or all the
                   funeral services...

CARL: You're so full of nostalgia...

GROM: One day he'll look back and he'll remember being nostalgic.

SIMON: I don't know which is worse. A church being turned into a private house. Or a pub. I used to come up here to look at the graves. Some are hundreds of years old. The names erased over time, secreted away by the sandpaper wind. I came here once with Suzie Wilson. We had a good look at one particular grave – she had 'loving wife of' imprinted on her back. But in reverse...

CARL: You've been around a bit, haven't you?

SIMON: Good boyo these days.

GROM: Wish I'd been around a bit.

CARL: Grom. You're standing on Mrs Hannah Rees. Beloved wife. Died 1906.

GROM: Sorry Mrs Rees!

TYPO: At Simon's father's fish and chip shop Doolally Sal stands in line waiting for half a portion of chips and a mushy pea fritter.

DOOLALLY SAL: 'Put a price on yourself,' my mother said. 'Meet a man who makes your life better.' Well I never did. The vicar's a widower now and I'm nothing but bones.

TYPO: The strippogram walks past the window.

DOOLALLY SAL: Look at her! Look at that tart! Tart!

TYPO: Penny Carter, in police shirt and garter ignores the catcalls and takes herself home alone to a romantic comedy she knows every word of, a bottle of sweet white wine and a three-pack of Ferrero Rocher.

STRIPPOGRAM: Sometimes I see a nice man. They look at my face, if they look at all. They think I'm too racy for mothers and doilies, best china and Angel cake, smiles and good manners on clock-ticking Sunday afternoons.

VIOLA: The old man is going away now.

GERAINT: Good. This isn't a refuge.

REVEREND: Amen.

TYPO: Up in Cae Du, nursing the hillside above the yellow glowing lamplight and satellite dish town, Ivor Thomas, son of Ivor, grandson of/

THOMAS: /Ivor. I loved my gampy.

TYPO: Unblocks a toilet, arm elbow deep, trying to loosen a loo roll some loser has lodged in a u-bend. The caravans laid out on the hill like coffins in a disaster zone.

THOMAS: It was a dairy farm back in the day. In the 70s Dad opened a caravan site on this field, on Cae Du. Nothing grew here because, rumour has it, when the Black Death came to the town, the victims were buried here. We don't tell the holidaymakers that though. But we do have signs up to discourage digging.

TYPO: In the cool late evening air small obese kids invade the village from the haunted caravan park. Dwayne Everett dribbles ice cream, shouts profanities, spits Wrigleys Permanent gum onto pavements, and throws stones at gulls.

DWAYNE: I hate you bloody gulls. Ha-ha! Aaargh! He crapped on me!!! He crapped on my head! Mammy!

TYPO: Dwayne doesn't know the gull, but the gull knows him. Dwayne swiped the eggs from its nest last week.

THOMAS: Day-trippers come here and they frown at the caravan site; a waste of lovely land they say. They've never been farmers - it's the hardest of lives, and caravans is worth more than cows.

TYPO: Locking up at the village store after a 14 hour shift, Mrs O'Shea, twice divorced, pulls down the shutters to stop vandals vandalising her emporium of Snapple juice, cheap electronic watches, warm chocolate and out of date sandwiches. As she heads home to make a hundred sweet welsh-cakes for the Lifeboat Stall at the Fun Day tomorrow, she sees her disgrace of a son swigging bottled beer by the cross on the town square.

MRS O'SHEA:	Clive! What you up to?
GROM:	Don't call me Clive, Mum!
MRS O'SHEA:	Clive was good enough for your grandfather.
GROM:	He had silver pocket watch and a handlebar moustache, Mum. He looked like a 'Clive'.
MRS O'SHEA:	You three ever going to grow up?
GROM:	It's Simon's stag night.
MRS O'SHEA:	I heard! Who'd have you, Simon Saddler?! You're nothing but a grin.
JILL JOG:	Got the girls.
LAZY LOTTIE:	Slept in a skip.
CAROL COMMODE:	Showed his b.t.m.
JILL JOG:	Rode naked into town on the roof of a bus.
LAZY LOTTIE:	On his eighteenth birthday.
CAROL COMMODE:	Who'd have him?
CARL:	Belle. He's marrying Belle.
MRS O'SHEA:	She must have taken leave of her senses.
BELLE:	I told him I was pregnant and he went down on one knee straight away. He looked odd down there: inappropriate. It was in a stream, see, under the aqueduct on the sunniest day ever. Some soldiers came abseiling over the top and Simon said he'd organised it, which of course he hadn't, but he made me laugh and I said 'I will...' coz I was in such a good mood. Engaged... it's for the best. Isn't it?
EVE:	I think she's mad. Can't tell her though. She's a smitten kitten.

BELLE:	He had wet knees and we made love in a field. We need more money though. Babies are expensive. At least he's got a job.
CARL:	In this small collection of streets, lanes and hiding places I am something of a catch. I worked hard in school, and worked my way up to assistant manager of the local DIY superstore. Others spent their time digging lug worms and flatting and drinking and setting snares, but not me. And yes, I really like Belle. Always have. I've known Simon since we were four years old. He had a good brain - we were first and second in class, him top in English, me in Maths. He always got the pretty girls; always told the best jokes. We had a fight once. We were nine years old. Someone put posters up around the school yard and cloak room. My mother had made me wear this tee-shirt/
YOUNG SIMON:	/What the hell's that?
YOUNG CARL:	What?
YOUNG SIMON:	That colour on your tee-shirt?
YOUNG CARL:	Pale red.
YOUNG SIMON:	It's not pale red. It's pink!! You poof!
YOUNG GROM:	Poof!
YOUNG CARL:	I'm not…
YOUNG SIMON:	Poof!
YOUNG CARL:	Don't call me that. We go fishing together.
YOUNG SIMON/GROM [effeminate]:	Fishing!
YOUNG CARL:	And push shopping trolleys in rivers.
YOUNG SIMON/GROM [effeminate]:	Pushing!
YOUNG CARL:	And we play football/

YOUNG SIMON/GROM [effeminate]:   /Football!

CARL: I won the scrap. But he won the war.

GROM: Shh... I've got Simon's phone! Who shall I text? 'Dear Belle, my sexy darling... I'd like to/

TYPO: /In Y-fronts and veil Belle faces her first challenge.

BELLE: EveeeennniiiinnngggPPPPPPooooooooosssssssssttttttt! Only one pence. Read all about it! Even though it's a month old! You sir, bet you haven't read about/

EVE: There's a ginger one there, ask him for a snog.

BELLE: I can't! Simon wouldn't like it... [to 'Ginger Man'] Sorry, sir, no offence. If I was single I'd be over like a shot...

TYPO: Handsome Dai, amateur DJ from the next village is handsome and playing records.

EVE: When they gave out handsome tablets he got the lot. Ask me out, Handsome Dai.

HANDSOME DAI: I'm Handsome Dai, son of the vet, amateur DJ and off to Uni... That girl's staring at me...

BELLE: He is gay, mind.

EVE: He's not! You're just jealous.

BELLE: He wanted to come on the hen night with us.

EVE: Are there any husbands out there? Ok, I'm looking for a gentleman, kind, considerate, great lover, good at DIY, faithful, single, doesn't need Viagra, no kids, handsome, a real sweetheart/

BELLE: /This is Wales you know.

HANDSOME DAI: This one's for the hen night! Let's see some moves!

BELLE/EVE/HENS: Whey!

[The 'hens' sing the chorus of Village People's 'YMCA', or similar.]

ALL *[sing]*:   *'YMCA*
                    It's fun to stay at the YMCA'

EVE: But he's so handsome!

[BELLE's text goes.]

BELLE: It's Simon. Bloody hell… read this, Eve.

EVE: That's a bit saucy!

BELLE: It's kinky is what it is!

GROM: Hee-hee!

EVE: No texting back, mind. It's a men-free night.

BELLE: But I want to see my daft boy. *[beat]* I'll text him.

VIOLA: Darling, when you've finished in the garden could you run up to the retail park?

GERAINT: Of course, darling…

VIOLA: I need to get some Ultramarine Blue, to finish the sky. And gas for the external heaters, and Monty and Jasmine want pizzas. Is it ok for them to have pizzas?

GERAINT: We are on holidays, darling.

VIOLA: Can't do any harm. Get fresh though, not frozen. And organic if you can.

GERAINT: Ok, darling.

VIOLA: And darling?

GERAINT: Yes darling?

VIOLA: Get me some olives?

GERAINT: Organic?

VIOLA: If you can, darling. Thank you.

GERAINT: Ok.

VIOLA: Yes, I think the sky needs more blue...

TYPO: It is 9 o'clock and the sounds of the disco at the rugby club can be heard across the town. It's happy hour, all drinks half price all night. The local rugby team disbanded a few years ago. Too drunk to field a team.

RUGBY LADS: *'Arrez zoomba zoomba zoomba*
                  Arrez zoomba zoomba zeh.'

TYPO: Yet the great songs of yore live on.

RUGBY LADS: *'We're going to the sunshine mountain*
                  Where the four winds blow
                  We're going to the sunshine mountain
                  To the place we used to go
                  Turn your back on all your troubles
                  Reach up to the sky
                  We're going to the sunshine mountain, you and I.'

TYPO: A few streets away in the dimmest of homes lives the brightest of men in this small town. In a caravan full of papers and books and draughts Professor Walford Richards, lecturer in Welsh History, smokes a pipe and tries to calm his overactive brain.

PROF RICHARDS: I'm an academic man, with a mind free to race through books and research. We are all tied to the past and a search for meaning. I looked across at my materialistic wife for years, always suppressing a sigh. I now realise that she was always suppressing the desire to stab me with a bread-knife.

MRS RICHARDS: He was so messy and distant. I took a lover. He moved out. But not very far. It was his decision.

PROF RICHARDS: I have no love of flesh and sweat.

TYPO: A rugged rumble brings consternation to the professor's brow as his romantic rival pulls up next to the careworn caravan in his JCB.

JCB: Everyone knows it's me in my yellow dinosaur; that's what our kid calls it. It's a bit weird having the 'ex' in the yard but I don't mind. He looks at me funny but it's ok. I'm bigger than he is. He looks at me like I'm worthless and whilst I'm not very educated, I'm on 35K a year and I won a JCB solo dancing competition in the Royal Welsh Show in 2005. His wife was neglected for years, but now she's taken care of… Oh yeah.

CAROL COMMODE: Shouldn't be allowed.

LAZY LOTTIE: Two men at once.

MRS RICHARDS: One for my body and one for my mind. To be honest though, my mind doesn't need much looking after.

TYPO: The professor found out about the affair when he was walking on the hill, near some burnt out cars. In one, still awaiting cremation, he thought children were playing. He went to see them; to tell them to be careful - joy-riders could roll another stolen saloon down the hill at anytime. The car squeaked and jolted/

PROF RICHARDS: /And inside was my wife having sex with the bloody JCB man. I knew it was him, by his Roman nose and a tattoo of a JCB on his buttock that rose and fell as he bulldozed away. I can honestly say she never looked so good. She looked like a whore, but a beautiful goddess-like whore. For a second there I thought I'd done something wrong, the way she looked at me. I couldn't take that, that look she had… There he was, with that bloody Roman nose. After a brief pause, they carried on carrying on…

MRS RICHARDS: I didn't mean to hurt him. But I know I did.

TYPO: Last minute preparations are being made for the fun day tomorrow. The bunting is up, the fireworks are ordered, the stands and stalls like a small medieval village rise on the pay-and-display car park. The lifeboat-men prepare for their demonstration and in the village hall the jumble sale sound of the Town Girls Kazoo Band practice their set for the Fun Day parade. They play some sort of tune. No-one recognises it. The town once had two brass bands, a choir, a string quartet and a jazz band. There is a jazz band playing tomorrow. They're coming by mini-bus from England. Prof Richards, who's organised the event, wrings his hands at changes of plans.

PROF RICHARDS: It's important that tradition survives. And not just for the sake of it. Our culture is under pressure. Choirs dwindling, barn dances dying out... *Dawnsio Werin* and *Noson Lawen*, all must be protected for the future. My wife used to like Ella Fitzgerald but is now quite a fan of someone called... name of *[remembers]*... 'Robbie Williams'. God help us all, but at least he's got a Welsh name...

[Robbie Williams' 'Rock DJ' blasts out.]

CARL: What time did they say they'd be here?

SIMON: Nine o'clock. Belle's never late.

GROM: Who's 'they'?

SIMON: The girls.

GROM: We're not meeting girls! This is supposed to be a stag do! It's tradition! Beer, wrestle, sleep in a skip!

TYPO: In the rugby club with its a collection of cups and jerseys and the board with the captains names on - Ophie Smith 1898, Iorwerth Davies 1899-1904... all the way up to last year, when the beer got the better of the rugby boys and the team disbanded for good, the appetites of the boys get bigger as the drinks get smaller, whilst up at Dylan's Tavern Theme Bar the girls dance a traditional communal jig as a subdued figure leaves, her work done for the evening.

STRIPPOGRAM: It was someone's 60th. He looked like my gramps, and was so drunk he could barely eat the banana from my cleavage. Someone else stepped in.

DRUNKEN DUNCAN: Only coz no-one was appreciating her.

STRIPPOGRAM: Someone always steps in. The cheery grippers with a soon-to-be extinguished light dancing in their yellow kind eyes are preferable to the rugby club scrum. The boys with their calloused hands, rough, grabbing at my flesh, taking revenge on me for their mothers not loving them enough. *[beat]* I call the pensioners 'grippers' coz they grip things. Banisters, chair backs, Zimmer frames… me. I like to think I'm providing a social service but really I jiggle for a living, I leave them unsatisfied. I leave them… unsatisfied.

TYPO: Simon gets a text message he does not expect.

SIMON: The Tavern… They're stopping there. Bloody hell boys, look at this text! That's a bit naughty! You can't deny that woman adores me.

CARL: A proper gentleman wouldn't show that to other people.

SIMON: Yeah, yeah…

CARL: Come on. Let's go there.

SIMON: Where?

CARL: The Tavern.

SIMON: Nah. It's too far mun. And we'll never get a cab.

CARL: More fun than this old dump. I'll drive… I want to see her… them. I want to see them. I'm ok.

GROM: Carl, you're barely able to speak.

CARL: I'm not going to talk to the car, I'm going to drive it. There's no-one about. Let's go.

TYPO: And off they go, bad boys into the night, drunk as skunks and looking
           for girls. The car speeds towards the village square, back towards the
           chapel. Grom singing his heart out, Carl concentrating, forehead
           furrowed. The lagers helped me too. I wrote bugger all but I'm not afraid
           anymore. And then out of the dark blue twitching night a skid, a crash
           and the chimes of midnight. Then silence. One thrown through the
           windscreen. One lost in the back. One out cold in the driver's seat. The
           one on the road rises very slowly, but steadily to his feet. He holds out
           his arms.

SIMON: How about this? How about this, eh?! I didn't mean what I said... I love
           her... *[beat - sings] 'Here comes the bride!' [beat]* I'm going to be a
           Dad. Me. How about that, eh? Simon Saddler pushing a pram, building a
           fort, watching him grow, making a mess, pushing him on a swing, going
           to rugby. And... things Dads do with their sons... Changing nappies...
           I'd even do that, I would, might not like it though... I'll get a good job...
           buy things... Scaletrix... Sorry Belle... and, um... I'll be a good Dad.
           True. Happy lad. Be happy. Lad... *[Big exhalation of breath.]* Phew!

[He collapses, dead. CARL opens his eyes.]

CARL: Sime? Grom? Say you're ok... Boys? *[beat]* Say you're ok. I'm sorry.
           Sime? Sime? *[beat]* Simon!

[Blackout.]

END OF ACT ONE

ACT TWO

RADIO:	'What's the situation?'
POLICE 1:	I've got the driver here. He's still breathing.
RADIO:	'Ambulance on its way.'
POLICE 1:	Soon as.
POLICE 2:	Sarge. Got another one. Must have been thrown clear.
POLICE 1:	Alive?*[beat]* Control, we may have another one.
POLICE 2:	No.
POLICE 1:	Cancel that. Just one survivor. The driver.
POLICE 2:	What about the one in the back?
POLICE 1:	Lost him.
POLICE 2:	He looked asleep.
CARL:	Police are coming back later to talk to me. After I've 'rested' apparently. I got out unscathed. Apparently. I had a dream. I was in a car, driving. I had two of my oldest mates with me. I crashed the car and now they're dead. And then I realised I hadn't woken up. Because I hadn't been asleep.
TYPO:	In the new light of morning Reverend Peacock walks his dachshund, Elijah, along the quay. He carries a pooper scooper and carrier bag and talks science to his canine congregation.
REVEREND:	There was a big explosion. And out of it came a living cell. And that living cell separated, and life began, and so every living thing is related back to that. So I am related to you, Elijah, and you to the grass you now urinate on. I'm not good with science, but it seems more plausible than the alternative. *[He looks up]* Sorry…
JILL JOG:	Have you heard the news?

REVEREND: What news, my dear?

TYPO: Carl stands outside Belle's house. The front door opens.

BELLE: It's seven in the morning. I thought you wouldn't even have got home by now. Did he behave?

CARL: Midnight finish.

BELLE: Sunglasses for your hangover, yeah?! We had a quiet one really… few dances… Eve asked out Handsome Dai… again. He said no. Again. Sorry we didn't make it to the rugby club though. Has he done something? What's the matter?

TYPO: Carl explains and Belle crumples in her hallway, pulling her tee-shirt down to cover her garter. Meanwhile, in his ramshackle balsa-thin caravan Professor Richards wonders how long he alone can keep up the lonely struggle to organise the Boat Club Fun Day.

PROFESSOR RICHARDS: Apathy won't cripple me. It's worth the hard work just to see all the town come out in the sun. I think…

TYPO: He opens the door to his recently ravaged wife.

MRS RICHARDS: I've brought you tea.

PROFESSOR RICHARDS: You haven't brought me tea in one year and three months.

MRS RICHARDS: You should give this place a lick of paint. I'll help you. *[beat]* Two boys died last night. In an accident. Up by the chapel. I don't know if it'll affect today… thought you should know.

PROFESSOR RICHARDS: That's… just… marvellous…

TYPO: Fast out of the general store Dwayne Everett, full of preservatives, scarpers clutching a Kinder Egg and tray of ten cheap electronic watches, one for each year of his delinquent life, that he has not paid for.

DWAYNE: I'm going to sell them on the beach like they do in Spain.

TYPO: But this morning Mrs O'Shea does not chase the thief.

MRS O'SHEA: The watches don't keep time anyway. A sales rep talked me into buying them. I had to open – people want bread and milk... newspapers. I sold out of flowers quite early.

TYPO: Up at the converted chapel PC Rees takes off his shoes.

PC REES: I like the way the light catches the railings. You're a good painter.

VIOLA: Oh really! Oh, you do have a good eye. You don't mind taking your shoes off, do you?

PC REES: No, no. Rules of the house. Quite understand.

VIOLA: You've got big feet.

PC REES: Why, thank you.

VIOLA: I was standing here, when I heard the crash. I was adding the ultramarine to the sky – do you see?

PC REES: Oh, right, yes. And that tree, is that the one out there?

VIOLA: You recognised it!

PC REES: It's my job to recognise things. I'm a police man.

VIOLA: My husband had just finished watching Newsnight. He was actually out there when it happened, he was taking a photograph. The moonlight was wonderful last night. Horrible to see those poor young men. Like broken birds. I didn't see you...?

PC REES: I didn't actually attend the scene. Traffic did. First exciting thing to happen here and I'm at home watching *Murder She Wrote*. Never mind...

TYPO: Bowling along with his red trolley, Stanley Postman, bald head and bow-legged, welcomes the morning with his usual sigh.

STANLEY: It's all junk and bills today. It saddens me deep in here that no-one hand crafts a letter of love at a leather-topped desk with blotting paper and ink-well any more. My post bag is bereft of fountain pen passion, of pressed flower paper, of perfumed pastel envelopes, of lavender, of rosy red lipstick kisses. And what will we hug close for warmth in a later loveless age? There's no shoebox crammed with loving correspondence - a red ribbon tied round its bulging middle - in our attics anymore. And attics! They've changed as well. They've been converted, or filled with lagging. As a small boy I went up my grandfather's attic – it was full of treasure. *[beat]* Of course, words of love are still communicated, but now are emailed and texted, and only survive until the hard drive dies.

JILL JOG: Have you heard the news?

STANLEY: 0% interest for six months? You've won a prize draw? APR down to 9.4% subject to status? I haven't steamed opened the mail mind. I just know.

[The Kazoo band pass, playing. SIMON appears.]

SIMON: Is that the sound of hell? I wondered where I was... Everywhere is colour and life, except... I don't quite know why I'm here. I thought I'd be somewhere else... or nowhere at all.

GROM: The copper said I was asleep. He cried, mun! Imagine that. A copper crying for me and my dead bones. There were three police cars. It's not the first time I've been surrounded by police, mind.

JILL JOG: He was still and small, right down behind the seat. Like a child asleep, the policeman said.

GROM: He cried! Well, I had to laugh. Nervous reaction I expect.

SIMON: The light is beautiful this morning. I walked round the town and saw an old man in a flat cap on a heavy wooden ladder painting his pebble dash magnolia and whistling; and a child on a scooter smiling like Christmas; and preparations for the Fun Day... I forgot last year, spent the day watching TV, but I was going to go to this one.

SIMONL   And up on the hill I saw a Jack Russell worrying two sheep until the two sheep got tired and chased the dog out of the field. I'm not normally up this early.I used to lie in the dark, hitting the snooze button for hours. I'd stay in bed until I was tired again. Lying in bed wondering why my life wasn't any better, yet not getting up to do anything about it. Always tomorrow…

[A passer-by passes by.]

              Morning!

[He's ignored.]

              It's a good morning. Yes it is.

GROM: Funny thing is, I didn't sleep much as a child. I was diagnosed with hyperactivity. I was a nuisance in class. They thought it was coz I was a shy genius bored by the lessons. But I wasn't a shy genius. I was just a nuisance. Look at this town. Like a kid's toy, all mine to play in. Sime, oh! [beat] Up here!

SIMON: Where?

GROM: Up here! Up here! I'm the king of the castle.

SIMON: It's not safe up there… that's why there's scaffolding.

GROM: You're right. Don't want to hurt myself do I?! I always wanted to climb to the top of this tower. I can see the whole town from here, cars like toys and people like dots. I saw your Dad…

SIMON: How was he?

GROM: Sad, he looked.

SIMON: Oh yeah…

GROM: Ah well, there's bugger all we can do about it now.

TYPO: Mr Saddler, owner of the chip shop, smelling of last night's wares, proud purveyor of all things deep fried recently moved the business upmarket by introducing plastic forks, wet wipes and mayonnaise sachets.

MR SADDLER: Apparently it's big in France. Mayo on chips. Had to make a stand, competition from the new curry house. I could see me in my son. This morning I can see me… Eager to please, to be polite, to be liked. He wanted to be my friend… He once asked me to take him on a tour of the town, tell him all my old haunts. Maybe I should have done. I went on a rugby trip to Paris in the late sixties. I was about his age. Young. And we got locked out of the hotel. So there we are, bit merry, midnight in Paris, all the lights, and we meet these women who invite us back to their house. We talk all night, though they couldn't speak English and we couldn't speak French, but… We had breakfast, French breakfast, croissant and chocolate like they do, and went on our way. Afterwards we all realised it was a brothel! He'd have liked that, my boy, Simon. His kind of story… yeah… I should have told him. I need to order some pasties. Maybe try some of those Jamaican ones. Spicier.

SIMON: What you been doing then?

GROM: I've been looking in bedroom windows. I've seen some things. No-one can see us, mun. This is much better than being alive. Couldn't do nothing then. Well, could, but always got caught. I saw that Penny Carter. Remember her?

SIMON: No.

GROM: The stripper. I saw her on the sand, looking to sea. There were some surfers out in the bay. I thought she was watching them but her eyes weren't. Someone had made one of those sculptures out of sea rope and driftwood and buoys and a training shoe. She was standing by it, skinny in the sun, fluttering like a flag and sad as half mast. Don't know why…

STRIPPOGRAM: When we were seven years old you sat behind me in Mr Jenkins class, and dropped pencils onto the floor and when you bent down to pick them up, I'd show you my knickers. You never looked at me after that, except once when I was stripping and you picked up my clothes and gave them back to me. You didn't know what to make of me, did you?

GROM: I remember her in school, she was going to be a ballerina. I liked her. Wrote her name on my satchel. On the inside.

SIMON: Did you see Belle?

GROM: No. What happened to you anyway? I didn't see.

SIMON: I got thrown into church hedge. Through the windscreen.

GROM: Handy for the funeral. Just dig a hole, like. Roll you in.

[The JOGGERS run past.]

SIMON: Morning ladies.

[They ignore him.]

GROM: They can't see you. Invisible we are!

SIMON: I know.

GROM: What I thought was/

SIMON: /I am not spying on women.

GROM: Right. *[beat]* You've thought tho'/

SIMON: /Well, yes, to be honest, but it wouldn't be right. That's not why we're here.

GROM: No… Not here to watch Eve Edwards getting dressed. And I didn't, not for long…

EVE: Handsome Dai turned me down. Again.

DOOLALLY SAL: Put a price on yourself.

EVE: I do. Too high.

DOOLALLY SAL: Do no harm to have a little sale once in a while.

SIMON: Have you seen Carl?

GROM: No. You?

CARL:	Time won't help me. 'In time', they say... but I walked by the slipway and I felt my friends were there, watching me. My head's in the shed.
DOOLALLY SAL:	There was adverts saying not to drink and drive. I saw them. Didn't those boys see them?
REVEREND:	Forgive yourself, my boy. If nothing else.
DRUNKEN DUNCAN:	Could have happened to anyone. I've done it, before I got banned, like.
MRS O'SHEA:	I feel for him.
STRIPPOGRAM:	Life's too short.
CARL:	They want to send a grief counsellor to see me. To counsel my grief. I don't want to recover. I'm the man who got drunk and killed his pals, by driving them into a graveyard wall. No excuses. No scapegoats. No skim of wet leaves. No badger taking a chance. No dangerous drunk coming at me on the wrong side of the road, because that was me. Too drunk. Too fast. Lost it on the bend by the square, hit the chapel wall. I remember a flash just before it happened...
BELLE:	If I hadn't asked him to join me... We had a rule, no texting coz you have to respond, but he sent me that text... I had to get back or he'd have felt daft. It was really saucy. He must have wanted to see me...
DOOLALLY SAL:	His fault. No-one else. Poor soul.
REVEREND:	Forgive him, Lord. If you're there.
MRS O'SHEA:	Asleep in the back they said. I hope it was quick. Accidents are what you fear as a mother. That knock, that whisper. Five times I've opened the door to a policeman. 'Is my boy dead?'
PC REES:	No, ma'am, we caught Grom/
MRS O'SHEA:	/Clive. His name is Clive.

PC REES:	Is it? I didn't know that! Well, well… Ok, we caught 'Clive' stealing from the charity box in the pub. How old is he?
MRS O'SHEA:	Twelve years old.
JILL JOG:	Remember when he stole the kestrel eggs?
MRS O'SHEA:	Thirteen.
LAZY LOTTIE:	Sprayed his name on the new village hall door?
MRS O'SHEA:	Fifteen.
CAROL COMMODE:	Sold amphetamine to surfers.
MRS O'SHEA:	Seventeen.
GROM:	It was only washing powder!
JILL JOG:	Smashed his father's car windscreen with a brick on the night his family was abandoned for a woman from Aberystwyth.
MRS O'SHEA:	Seven years old.
PC REES:	I have some bad news.
MRS O'SHEA:	Is my boy dead?
CARL:	Simon said something, distracted me… No. Not anybody else to blame. Just me. Only doing forty. Too fast though. Too drunk. There was a flash … What was that? We only wanted to meet the girls. Well, I wanted to - 'Don't marry him, Belle.' My final pitch. My big best man's best speech, one week early. Makes a change from stories about exes and curry houses.
BELLE:	But it's all arranged, and I love him and he loves me. And you're the best man… This is a joke isn't it? Isn't it?
CARL:	Yes, Belle. My sense of humour. Bit obscure…

PC REES:	Sorry, Mr Saddler.
MR SADDLER:	I had to open. Did I ever tell you about the time?/
PC REES:	/Car's on double yellows, got any curry sauce?
MR SADDLER:	Curry sauce? Right…
PC REES:	And a saveloy.
MR SADDLER:	Right… Oh, and if you see Carl tell him/
CARL:	/I don't want forgiveness.
ALL:	He's forgiven.
CARL:	NO!
JILL JOG:	She opened the store this morning.
LAZY LOTTIE:	She never!
CAROL COMMODE:	I bought bleach and she said nothing.
REVEREND:	Help him, Lord. With your grace
DOOLALLY SAL:	We lie down in life and rarely leave a mark.
STRIPPOGRAM:	What was he like? I didn't know him well. I'm going to give up stripping.
DRUNKEN DUNCAN:	I once drank 15 pints and crashed into a ditch. Slept in the ditch, got home and forgot about it. Until now.
JILL JOG:	I said, 'Sorry to hear…' and bought Diet Coke, Weight Watchers vegetable bake and a Snickers as a treat.
LAZY LOTTIE:	And she never said anything?
JILL JOG:	Just gave me the change. I hovered like, in case she wanted to tell me more.

LAZY LOTTIE:	Seen them bunches of flowers at the crash site?
CAROL COMMODE:	She sold them. Making money out of her son's death. It's terrible.
LAZY LOTTIE:	Some people don't know how to behave.
STRIPPOGRAM:	What was he like? I never knew him at all.
CAROL COMMODE:	Drunk he was, that Carl boy. You know him? Tidy family, live up in the big semi with the stained glass window on the landing. I went there when I was a kid. First house I'd ever seen with a tele upstairs.
JILL JOG:	Almost pity him.
CARL:	DON'T PITY ME!

[SIMON and GROM wander by. CARL feels something.]

CARL:	Simon? Grom?
LAZY LOTTIE:	Have you heard? Drunk they were.
CARL:	Have you heard?
CAROL COMMODE:	Have you heard? Lucky to be alive.
LAZY LOTTIE:	Hi… um… sorry to hear…
MRS O'SHEA:	Aye.
LAZY LOTTIE:	Have you got any Ideal Milk?
JILL JOG:	Have you heard?
CARL:	YES! I'M THE LUCKY ONE!
MRS O'SHEA:	I'll have to get some from the warehouse. Thursday.
LAZY LOTTIE:	Oh, it's just Jessie's birthday. She's two… having a little party.

MRS O'SHEA:	I've got fresh things that had to be sold. Ok? But I've got a girl in this afternoon. Because then I'm selling welsh-cakes for the lifeboat, just so you know!
LAZY LOTTIE:	Sorry I mentioned it.
MRS O'SHEA:	Me too.
GROM:	I want a smoke. I'm glad about this. Everything's different. Exciting. What shall we do?
SIMON:	Has it occurred to you that we're not supposed to be here? Unless it's for a reason.
GROM:	Nope. I don't want to get all philosophical just coz I've died and yet still seem to be here. Life's too short. And it was!
SIMON:	Do you think you wasted your life?
GROM:	I think I had a life and it was crap, and now I'm dead and it's better.
SIMON:	Better?
GROM:	Yeah! Now I don't have to do anything for anybody… If I want to swear or stare at women's chests or run around naked no-one can stop me.
SIMON:	You've thought this through then.
GROM:	Yes. BOLLOCKS!! Come on Sime, it'll do you good. BOLLOCKS! Great! Shout it out!
SIMON:	Life was great. This isn't. Don't you feel down?
GROM:	I can only feel what I feel, and it wasn't great, mun. It was dull. You said so. All the time.
SIMON:	I didn't appreciate it. We had everything.
GROM:	BOLLOCKS!! What did we have?

SIMON:	We could swim in the sea every day.
GROM:	BOLLOCKS!! Did you?
SIMON:	Watch the baby otters in the estuary.
GROM:	BOLLOCKS!! Bore me to death/
SIMON:	/And the seals off the headland.
GROM:	Since when were you interested in any of that animal stuff?
SIMON:	Since now! Ok? Since I haven't got it anymore. I'm angry. I could have learnt the names of the sea birds, and the constellations... known where the fish are, like my Grandad did – he could smell them and load his wheelbarrow with fish before anyone else had baited their rods.
GROM:	You're bloody miserable you are!
SIMON:	Yeah! I am, ok? I am bloody miserable!

PROFESSOR RICHARDS *[on tannoy]*:

I declare the Annual Fun Day OPEN!

[SOUND – Brass Band]

PROFESSOR RICHARDS *[on tannoy]*:

Excuse me!

[SOUND - Brass Band continue]

Excuse me!!

[SOUND – Brass Band stop]

We'll start with a minute's silence. For the young men.

GROM:	For us? Cool! Do we have to do it?

SIMON:	I'm not aware of the protocol.
GROM:	Proto-what?
SIMON:	Never mind.
GROM:	Your problem is that you're romantic. You got a book of stars at home but have you read it? You have a beer, then it's, 'There's the Plough', and 'Orion's Belt' if we're lucky.
SIMON:	I was going to learn them.
GROM:	I bet all your beloved ancestors didn't know the names of them.
SIMON:	They might have.
GROM:	Ok… there's the pint glass, there's the snooker triangle and that one looks like… an unicorn.
SIMON:	Shut up…
GROM:	You got to know yourself. Number one – lazy. Number two - you watched too much daytime TV… You wasted your life on makeover shows and obscure sports and now you're all maudlin and full of, 'What ifs?'
SIMON:	I wanted simple things. Get married. Have kids. Get a good job. Go to Disneyland.
GROM:	You didn't love her. You hate kids. You're unemployable, and Disneyland is someone else's dream.
GERAINT:	We went to Disneyland.
VIOLA:	Geraint planned it meticulously.
GERAINT:	Went like a dream.
VIOLA:	He bribed the rep. *[beat]* Is this what they call a 'Fun Day'. A bouncy castle and a scruffy fair?

PROFESSOR RICHARDS *[on tannoy]*:

> Thank you to the lifeboat crew for that demonstration. And now, an exhibition of JCB dancing by the man who stole my wife, and because of whom I now live in a battered caravan... Bloody Roman nose...

GERAINT: Fancy living here all the time.

VIOLA: I'd go mad. What's he actually doing in that machine?

PROFESSOR RICHARDS *[on tannoy]*:

> Same old moves... Same old tricks... bor-ing...

TYPO: Kazoo and jazz band, stilt walker and crooked house, merry-go-round, hot dog van, lifeboat, fire engine, six boats, three canoes and a dinghy keep the children eyes-wide, happy and candy-floss faced as the adults drink warm beer from plastic glasses in the dreary summer air. Drunken Duncan under the influence takes a nap in a small rowing boat. Rugby boys out for mischief push the boat out into the fast ebbing tide.

RUGBY LADS: Hooray!

TYPO: I decide I need some fresh air and exercise and join the rugby lads...

RUGBY LADS: Hooray!

TYPO: Detox tomorrow.

RUGBY LADS: Boo!

DRUNKEN DUNCAN: Help! I'm afloat!

GROM: You don't want to be in Disneyland. You're better off here with me. We're the same, we are.

SIMON: We are not the bloody same! I want to be on my own. Go away.

GROM: We are. Face it, you're just like me, except you think you're better coz you're more intelligent. You wasted your life and now you're wasting your death. Need a ciggie...

DRUNKEN DUNCAN: Help me!!

PROFESSOR RICHARDS [on tannoy]:

There we are, JCB dancing. Fantastic. I really mean it... [barely audible] Bastard! [beat] Could the teams for the tug-of-war competition make their way to the strip of grass by the quay.

SIMON: I was about to get married. Things would change then. I miss her. I do.

DRUNKEN DUNCAN [further away]: Help!!

GROM: I heard what you said in the car.

SIMON: They were just words.

GROM: 'I don't want to marry her'...?

SIMON: Just words.

GROM: You know Carl's always liked her...

SIMON: Shut up! I miss her, right? I miss what she knew about me. How to rub my feet. What shirts I liked. She saw through my games, she calmed me down...

BELLE: The inside of my head is like a bomb's gone off in a library; can't concentrate. I concentrate on concentrating... I fail.

SIMON: I loved Belle, I did. I know what I said... but I did. She was uncomplicated. She had a built in bullshit detector. If I said, 'You're wonderful', she'd go –

BELLE: Why?

SIMON: And I'd smile, and not use words, and she'd know. She untangled me. Maybe I'm supposed to help her now. But what can I do? She can't hear me. She can't see me.

BELLE: You think too much/

SIMON: /Too much and not enough.

PROFESSOR RICHARDS *[on tannoy]*:

          Last call for the tug-of-war.

TYPO: The tug-of-war competition is cancelled. The rugby team is too drunk.

RUGBY LADS: Hooray!

TYPO: Trousers are taken off and thrown around for fun. Change and lighters fall from pockets. Behinds are shown to chip-eating day-trippers.

MR SADDLER: Mayonnaise with them?

PROFESSOR RICHARDS *[on tannoy]*:

          Is it just me taking this seriously?! Do you know how much work I put in? DO YOU?!!

TYPO: Old couples in parked cars drink tea from thermos flasks. Soon they will drive away having never left their vehicles. Brash boys muscle and preen and bejewelled girls lobster in the sun and out in the bay Drunken Duncan fades into the horizon, a big man in a tiny boat.

DRUNKEN DUNCAN *[very far away]*:   I'll never drink again.

JILL JOG: Liar!

CARL: He had the best girl in the village, he did… and he didn't really want her.

SIMON: I do. I did…

CARL: He'd never take care of her. I would have. But that New Years' Eve he came along with his slick smirk and la-di-da swagger and took her like a leaf from a tree. I was playing the long game. Nothing had happened but we'd crossed the road the day he made his move, and I put my hand like this... on the small of her back like this, *[does it to BELLE]* and she smiled and said...

BELLE: Thank you.

CARL: That was good wasn't it? Later, at the party I was all ready to, I don't know... try and hold her hand I suppose... and she arrives at the door. At the door with him.

SIMON: I didn't know.

CARL: They'd met at the rugby club and the game was over... She smiled at me as she arrived, but I knew. I stayed in the party all night, all false and smiling out here, but cold and faking in here. He knew it too. Bloody knew it.

BELLE: Hi.

CARL: I can't stay in. Don't run away.

BELLE: I needed to be with people, strangers, anyone... I'm like a shadow in search of sunshine.

CARL: Simon told me how much he loved you last night.

BELLE: Did he? He always laughed when he said nice things to me. Always a cheeky grin, even when he proposed. He'd say, 'Love you loads', or 'Love you lots', never, 'I. Love. You.' And he'd say 'ditto' if I said I loved him.

CARL: He said it last night. That he loved you. *[beat]* I always liked you.

BELLE: No, Carl.

CARL: I can say things today. Put things right.

SIMON: He kissed her. He bloody kissed her! What you doing mate?! And she didn't push him away!

BELLE: Carl, you're in shock. You should be at home. You should be
                somewhere else. Anywhere else. But not here.

CARL: What we need to do is ride this out, get ourselves through it…
                promise me. Promise me you'll be ok. You're lovely, Belle.
                Lovely.

TYPO: Simon stares as Carl starts to go. Belle rubs her belly. Simon puts
                his arms around her. She doesn't feel him.

SIMON: Remember me. I'll remember you.

BELLE: Carl? I'll… speak to you… soon?

[They share a moment. SIMON moves away.]

PROFESSOR RICHARDS *[on tannoy]*:

                I don't have to do this you know. Next year organise your own
                sodding fun day. Bastards!

VIOLA: Not many boats.

GERAINT: No fishermen anymore.

VIOLA: Why do they bother?

GERAINT: Tradition.

VIOLA: Look, there's Jasmine and Monty.

[They hear a sound – a jet-ski.]

MRS O'SHEA *[shouting over the noise]*:

                All home made. Welshcakes and Maids Of Honour. Fresh today.
                All proceeds to the lifeboat-men.

VIOLA: May I try one? *[beat]* Bit sweet. I'll leave them thanks.

GROM: Hiya Mum! It's me. I messed up. Again.

MRS O'SHEA:	I liked him when he was little. Till he was seven. Can't blame his dad leaving… Then this… personality arrived. This noisy, brattish… and the smoking. He smoked when he was 10. Rollies. He always smelt like an old man. A noisy brattish old man. Then the dope and then dirty magazines under his bed. I couldn't say anything, we sold them in the shop. But I stopped then. He used to nick things all the time. I'd tell him, 'Tell me what you want, sweets whatever, and I'll get them for you.' He never listened. He just nicked.
GROM:	I didn't want to trouble you.
MRS O'SHEA:	I'm gonna miss the sod. The stupid time-wasting sod. The stupid, 'I'll be around for dinner at 2', and then turn up at 5 all beery and smoky and late. He never had any luck.
EVE:	Hiya babes.
BELLE:	Carl kissed me.
EVE:	That's not right…
BELLE:	It shouldn't be right. My head told me that. You tell me that. You're right. I think...
EVE:	You're in shock. You don't know what to feel.
BELLE:	You thought I should have chosen him instead of Simon didn't you?
EVE:	Carl was lovely.
BELLE:	You said dull.
EVE:	Dull as in 'safe'.
BELLE:	Simon wasn't safe.
EVE:	Simon was loud. As loud as a bus-load of Brummies.
BELLE:	Snored like a goods train.

EVE: Picked his nose.

BELLE: Chewed his toes and ate the nails.

EVE: Talked/

BELLE: /Over me. Sweated in bed.

EVE: You could have done worse though.

BELLE: Could have done better.

CARL: When we were in the car that night, and we're on his stag do and she loves him and she's out on her night and we're having a laugh and we get in my car... Which was stupid... and he says as we come down by the old chapel, he says, 'You know what, mate... I don't want to marry her!' He bloody said it!

SIMON: I didn't mean it.

CARL: He said it all bravado. For effect. But I couldn't believe it. 'I don't want to marry her.' Then some flash... Next thing, bang... Bloody bang... BANG!

SIMON: I can't talk to people. I can't touch people. Why am I here? What's the point of existence if you can't affect people? Help them?

GROM: Sime?

SIMON: What?

GROM: Penny? The Strippogram girl? She was crying for me! I heard her tell one of the joggers by the old pump! One of them was having a go or something about, 'He was a waste of space', and all that, which is fair enough, but... Penny said –

STRIPPOGRAM: He had kind eyes.

GROM: Kind eyes! Me! What do you think?

SIMON: WHY ARE WE STILL HERE?

GROM: I thought you'd have chilled out in my absence. But no… STOP
             THINKING, MUN!

SIMON: There should be a million other dead people wandering around,
             yeah? Where are they?! It's just us. You. And I.

GROM: 'Kind eyes!' she said.

SIMON: We should be gone! We shouldn't be able to see Penny bloody
             Carter saying you had kind eyes, or, I dunno… Carl kissing
             Belle…

GROM: He what?

SIMON: Kissed Belle. It's ok, she didn't kiss him back. Having said that,
             she had this look… this bloody look!

GROM: Aw, maan! He shouldn't have done that.

SIMON: I'm worried about him. Even though I wanted to punch him. He
             won't do anything daft, will he?

GROM: He's Carl isn't he? He doesn't do daft. *[beat]* I feel cold.

SIMON: Me too.

TYPO: Dusk draws a muslin mist over the town. Smoke from barbecues
             and bonfires warms the evening air and the lads in hoodies now
             cuss and jostle, and girls in micro skirts giggle in despair. Music
             from the fair-rides ring out across the mudflats, and the tired
             trickle tide turns once more.

[SOUND – fairground]

             Skimming across the sea a lone jet-ski races for no good reason.

JILL JOG: Bloody jet-skis!

LAZY LOTTIE: So noisy!

VIOLA: That isn't Jasmine.

TOWNSFOLK:	Jasmine?!
GERAINT:	That isn't Monty.
TOWNSFOLK:	Monty?!!
VIOLA:	Someone's stolen a jet-ski! Our bloody jet-ski!
CAROL COMMODE:	Fireworks!
JILL JOG:	Look kids!

[SOUND – fireworks.]

CHILDREN:	Hooray!
BELLE:	He's going too fast.
EVE:	He's heading for the cliff. Who is it?
BELLE:	Oh no… it's Carl. It must be Carl.
REVEREND:	Slow down!

[SOUND – fireworks.]

CHILDREN:	Hooray!
DOOLALLY SAL:	Bloody noise! Sorry Lord, for swearing.
GERAINT:	I say! That's ours!
STRIPPOGRAM:	Way too fast.
GROM:	Is that Carl?

[The SOUND of a jet-ski hitting a cliff. SIMON and GROM make their way to the front of the crowd.]

SIMON:	What are you playing at, mate?
GROM:	If he's dead, will he join us?

SIMON:	If he turns up here, I'll kill him.
GROM:	Maybe we were supposed to help him, or something…
SIMON:	What could we do, Grom? We couldn't speak to him? He couldn't see us…
TYPO:	And in a hospital a drama is played out as doctors try and stabilize the limp body of Captain Carl, full of regret and wires and drips as he rings the bell at death's door.
REVEREND:	God help this poor man, Oh Lord/
DOOLALLY SAL: /	In your mercy/
REVEREND:	/Hear our prayer.
TYPO:	Night falls in, the fair shudders to a silence, and the town fades into the hill once more. The lifeboat picked up Drunken Duncan half way to Tenby in a state of mild delirium.
DRUNKEN DUNCAN:	I need a drink.
TYPO:	In the tightly shuttered dimly lit bar of the Old Red Lion the last drunken boyos are ushered out. Two men remain… no-one asks them to leave… because no-one sees them.

[As before GROM plays the imaginary matchbox game.]

GROM:	Two fingers… Me.

[He mimes drinking two fingers of beer.]

SIMON:	You're going to play it on your own?
GROM:	Won't be the first time.
SIMON:	With no drink or matchbox?

[GROM's eyes wander to the audience. He speaks confidentially to SIMON.]

GROM:	Weird, mun… Sort of just sitting there looking at us.

59

SIMON: Yeah…

GROM: Are they ghosts? Do they know why we're here?

SIMON: Don't know.

GROM: Do they know why they're here?

[GROM slyly indicates an audience member.]

That one… looks a bit… simple.

TYPO: The already dim light flickers…

GROM: I don't want to go.

[GROM passes SIMON the imaginary matchbox. GROM is insistent. SIMON reluctantly takes it. GROM indicates to him to play. SIMON throws it. Pause. GROM watches expectantly. SIMON smiles.]

SIMON: It landed in my pint.

GROM: Yes! The rules state, sir, that you have to drink that pint down in one.

CARL: Rules are rules.

GROM: Aw, shit…

SIMON: You are not dead. You have no right to be here.

CARL: I'm in a bad way, apparently.

SIMON: Then you've got to fight this! You got to pull through. Doctors said 50-50/

GROM: /Good odds/

CARL: /I don't want to pull through. I can't live with what I've done. People judging me… Can't take the pressure of being the lucky one. The one who survived.

SIMON: You selfish little git! We've got no bloody choice here but you've
                got a chance to have a life. If I had just half a chance... What were
                you thinking? In front of everyone, there were kids watching,
                yeah? People are very upset. Cheer them up with a miracle. Go on,
                resurrect yourself.

CARL: I want to be here, with you.

SIMON: /Nah! It's really bleak here, Carl. AND WE'RE VERY
                SCARED!!

CARL: Why are you still here?

GROM [re. SIMON]:   Don't start him on that! He's been banging on about it all
                    day... Why are we still here?!

CARL: I felt you two were still around. Is it just you two?

[GROM subtly indicates the audience.]

GROM: There's a few others. Don't know who they are. Rum bunch.
                They're just staring...

SIMON: We're not anywhere anymore. Feel my hand.

CARL: Freezing.

SIMON: And the light flickers and we don't know if or when it's going
                to go out.

GROM: And beer tastes terrible when you're dead, and if you see girls
                in their underwear... well... *[indicates his crotch]* nothing
                happens.

SIMON :   You've got a second chance. Go back. Smell the flowers enjoy the
                mornings, the characters of the town, sunsets, colours, the kiss of a
                girl... Go on! You haven't got much time.

GROM: You always had to go home early!

CARL: I know. I always envied you two. Under the lamp post talking
                complete tosh long into the night.

SIMON: Changing the world. How we were going to leave our mark. We wanted you to stay then, but now we want you to sod off! We're fading mate… like names on weather-beaten gravestones – me, Simon Saddler.

GROM: Me, Clive O'Shea.

CARL: I forgot it was Clive.

GROM: It was my grandfather's name.

SIMON: Go and learn the constellations.

GROM: Keep off the booze and the fags.

SIMON: Make a good life for yourself.

GROM: Tell them all I apologise.

SIMON: Read more books.

GROM: Buy loads of stuff in my mum's shop.

SIMON: Look after Belle…

[beat. Awkward silence.]

            And my kid.

[beat. SIMON nods.]

CARL: Ok.

SIMON: And tell my Dad that I… you know. Now get lost.

GROM: And tell Penny Carter… nothing. No, that I thought she was nice. Really nice.

CARL: Ok.

GROM: Will you?

CARL: Yeah. I will. Ok, lads, I'll/

GROM/SIMON: /GO!!!

[He nods and goes.]

GROM: Sime, oh!

SIMON: What?

GROM: I know why we're here! We're angels, aren't we? Seems to be an explanation, like good angels.

TYPO: The light flickers yet again.

SIMON: See that?

GROM: That's what we had to do! Save his life! That was our job, why we didn't go. We're bloody angels, mun!

SIMON: The light keeps flickering.

GROM: We're still here though, aren't we? So, we must have more things to do. Coz we're good at being angels. First challenge, we met it. No probs. I'd like a pair of those big wings. Oi! You up there! I said I'd like a pair of big wings! And a guitar thing!

SIMON: Lute.

GROM: Aye! And one of them! And a big white cloak and a nice cloud to sit on. And a book of the chords coz I'm not very musical. And a halo! All new and gold. Size large.

SIMON: Who are you talking too?

GROM: Him, isn't it! I don't want to be hedging my bets at this stage. Do you think there is a Pearly Gates?

SIMON: I don't think there is a better world than the one we just left.

[The light flickers. The men react.]

GROM: Wish I had another chance. Walk down the street and hear that I'm
               a good bloke. *[beat]* Just walking down a street even... Carl's
               lucky, isn't he?... Lucky, lucky... *[beat]* I'm jabbering a bit.
               Aren't I? Jabbering? Sorry... *[beat]* Game of pool?

[CARL appears – SIMON and GROM can't believe it]

CARL: I didn't make it.

*[The light flickers. They all look up, then at each other. The lights fade slightly. They
embrace.]*

GROM *[singing]*: *'We're going to the sunshine mountain'*

[The other joins in, quietly, but firmly. The light fades a little more.]

               'Where the four winds blow.
               We're going to the sunshine mountain
               To the place we used to go-oh-oh-oh'

[Blackout. They've gone. Small blue light up on TYPO – a bit worse for wear.]

TYPO: The words didn't flow so I looked round the town for inspiration,
               for drama... for one luminous strand. I wrote buggerall, but won a
               goldfish and called him Dylan. I went to someone's house and fell
               asleep on the sofa. *[beat]* But I've made loads of notes... and told
               everyone about it... and got some good ideas written somewhere...
               da iawn to me.

[Searches pockets.]

               Somewhere. On a bit of paper... Honest, I haven't been doing
               buggerall... *[chuckles]* Every time... *[can't find paper]* Start
               again tomorrow... *[Looks up.]* I can see the plough... and...
               [Searches] Orion's belt... where is it? Is that it? Yeah... What's
               that one?

[He stares at the sky. TOWNSFOLK appear and look to the sky.]

TOWNSFOLK: The Water Carrier. The Lesser Dog. Perseus. The Crab.
The Hunting Dogs. The Furnace. The Shield. Hercules.
Ursa Minor. The Compass. The Great Bear. Ursa Major.
The Peacock. The Fishes. The Crane. The Altar. The Sea
Goat. Andromeda. The Flying Fish.

[beat]

The Unicorn.

The End